Fairy Realm

book 8

the water sprites

FAIRY REALM

The Charm Bracelet

The Flower Fairies

The Third Wish

The Last Fairy-Apple Tree

The Magic Key

The Unicorn

The Star Cloak

ROWAN OF RIN

Rowan of Rin

Rowan and the Travelers

Rowan and the Keeper of the Crystal

Rowan and the Zebak

Rowan and the Ice Creepers

Fairy Realm

the water sprites

book 8

EMILY RODDA

ILLUSTRATIONS BY RAOUL VITALE

www.harperchildrens.com

Library of Congress Cataloging-in-Publication Data
Rodda, Emily.
  The water sprites / Emily Rodda ; illustrations by Raoul Vitale.— 1st ed.
    p.   cm. — (Fairy realm ; bk. 8)
  Summary: During her most recent visit to the Fairy Realm, Jessie inadvertently allows a baby fairy to be captured by water sprites who want to hold the child captive until their missing moon stone is returned.
  ISBN-10: 0-06-077761-3 — ISBN-10: 0-06-077762-1 (lib. bdg.)
  ISBN-13: 978-0-06-077761-6 — ISBN-13: 978-0-06-077762-3 (lib. bdg.)
  [1. Fairies—Fiction. 2. Water spirits—Fiction. 3. Moon stones—Fiction.] I. Vitale, Raoul, ill. II. Title.
PZ7.R5996Wat 2005   2005006825
[Fic]—dc22   CIP
                                                                  AC

Typography by Karin Paprocki
1 2 3 4 5 6 7 8 9 10
❖
First Edition

CONTENTS

1. An Invitation   1

2. The Daisy Trail   13

3. The Finding Pool   23

4. Jessie's Good Deed   33

5. The Party by the Stream   43

6. The Tale of the Moon Stone   55

7. The Bargain   65

8. A Discovery   75

9. Race Against Time   85

10. Just as It Was   95

CHAPTER ONE

An Invitation

Jessie fastened her charm bracelet around her wrist and checked her reflection in the mirror. Her green eyes were sparkling. Her golden red hair shone against the rich blue of her new dress. She looked happy and excited, and no wonder! It was a sunny Saturday afternoon, and she was going to a party. Not an ordinary party, either, but a party in the magical world of the Realm.

The charm bracelet jingled softly as Jessie picked up the gold-speckled leaf lying beside her hairbrush. When she'd found the leaf on her desk a couple of days before, she'd thought at first that it was quite ordinary. She thought the breeze had blown it through her open window.

She'd never seen a leaf just like it before, but that wasn't surprising. The garden of Blue Moon, her grandmother's old house in the mountains, was filled with unusual trees and bushes. Though she and her mother had been living with Granny for over a year, Jessie was still discovering plants that were new to her.

But when she picked up the speckled leaf, she suddenly saw that there was something strange about it. The yellow speckles were in straight lines, set tidily one above the other. Jessie peered at them closely. And then she realized that the speckles were words! The leaf was covered in tiny yellow writing.

Jessie smiled as she remembered how astonished and delighted she'd been as she read the leaf's message for the first time.

Princess Jessie! The village of Lirralee invites you to baby Jewel's Welcome Party on Saturday afternoon. The party begins at three o'clock and ends when the birds go to bed. There will be music, dancing, games, and lots of food. Please come!

On the other side of the leaf there was another message, in different handwriting.

Hope you can come, Jessie. Giff and Maybelle are invited, too. Be at my place at 2:30 and we can all go together. Lirralee is my old home village. Everyone is longing to meet you. Love, Patrice.

Jessie had been very relieved to read that note. She had no idea where Lirralee was, but with her friends Patrice the palace housekeeper, Giff the elf, and Maybelle the miniature horse to guide her, she wouldn't get lost.

She glanced at the clock on her bedside table and was startled to see that it was after two o'clock. Time had flown. If she didn't hurry, she'd be late. She grabbed the gift she'd wrapped in silver paper, and hurried out of her room to find her grandmother.

Voices were floating from the kitchen. Jessie

sighed as she recognized the chirping tones of Mrs. Tweedie, the next-door neighbor.

What a nuisance! Mrs. Tweedie was a very curious woman. If she saw Jessie heading for the bottom of the Blue Moon garden dressed in party clothes, she'd ask all sorts of questions.

Jessie hesitated, wondering if she should just slip out the front door without saying good-bye. Her mother was out for the day, and Granny would understand.

"I'm so upset!" Mrs. Tweedie wailed. "I was terribly fond of that ring. It was my mother's."

"I'm sure you'll find it, Louise," Granny said soothingly. "It's probably just fallen—"

"No!" Mrs. Tweedie insisted. "It was on my bedside table, in a little crystal dish. I remember *perfectly*. I put it there before I did the washing. I *always* put it there. That Wiseman person who came to clean the windows took it. I *know* he did."

Jessie's eyes widened, and she felt heat rush into her face. Mr. Wiseman was the father of her friend Sal. He was a kind, cheerful man, always full of jokes and fun, just like Sal. What was Mrs. Tweedie saying about him?

She rushed into the kitchen. Granny and Mrs. Tweedie turned to look at her.

"Is that a new outfit, dear?" asked Mrs. Tweedie, her sharp little nose twitching as she looked Jessie up and down. "I don't think I've seen it before. It's very pretty. Are you going to a party?"

"Yes," Jessie said breathlessly. "But, Mrs. Tweedie, I couldn't help hearing what you were saying about Mr. Wiseman just now, and—"

Mrs. Tweedie's face grew solemn. "It's not very nice, I know," she said. "I hate to accuse anyone, but facts are facts. I can't go to the police—I mean, the man will just deny he took my ring, won't he? But I know he did it, and it's only right to warn people about him."

"Louise, believe me, Alf Wiseman is no thief!" Granny said very firmly. "He's been in and out of Blue Moon for years—ever since he started his window-cleaning business. He's as honest as the day is long."

"Of course he is!" Jessie exclaimed. "He's my friend's dad. I know him really well."

Mrs. Tweedie looked at her sorrowfully. "I *am* sorry, dear," she said. "But, sadly, people aren't always what they seem."

"Jessie, you'd better go, or you'll be late," Granny said as Jessie opened her mouth to argue. "You'll have to run as it is."

"Don't tell me you're *walking* to the party, dear?" cried Mrs. Tweedie as Jessie hurried to the door. "In your nice dress and shoes? No, no. Come on, I'll drive you."

"No!" Jessie exclaimed, horrified. "I mean, thank you, but it isn't far. I don't need a lift."

"It's no trouble!" said Mrs. Tweedie. "I must go, anyway. I just popped in for a minute to see if your grandmother wanted anything at the supermarket."

And to spread rumors about Mr. Wiseman, Jessie thought furiously. But the anger was driven from her mind as Mrs. Tweedie picked up her handbag and car keys from the kitchen table and bustled to join her at the door.

"Now, where's this party? Which street?" Mrs. Tweedie asked brightly.

Panic-stricken, Jessie glanced at her grandmother.

"What a shame you have to go so soon, Louise," Granny said calmly. "I thought you might like to see Robert's studio today. But if you don't have time . . ."

Mrs. Tweedie's eyebrows shot up. For months she'd been hinting that she wanted to see where Jessie's grandfather, Robert Belairs, had painted the fairy pictures that had made him famous.

"Oh!" she exclaimed, glancing from Granny to Jessie. "Well, I . . ."

"You stay, Mrs. Tweedie," Jessie said rapidly. "I'll be fine, really. Bye, Granny."

And thanks, she added silently, as she closed the door behind her. She darted into the shade of the trees behind the house, and began running toward the tall, clipped hedge at the bottom of the garden.

Seeing Grandpa's studio will put Mrs. Tweedie in a good mood, she thought as she ran. Maybe

7

then Granny will be able to convince her that Mr. Wiseman couldn't have stolen her ring. Oh, I hope so.

She could just imagine Mrs. Tweedie twittering over the paintings stacked against the studio walls.

"Oh, they're really *marvelous*," Mrs. Tweedie would be saying to Granny, as if Granny didn't know. "So magical, yet so *lifelike*. You'd swear he'd really *seen* the things he painted!"

"Yes, people often say that," Granny would agree mildly. And she'd listen with a smile while Mrs. Tweedie went on and on.

Because only Jessie shared Granny's secret. Only Jessie and Granny knew that Robert Belairs really *had* seen the things he'd painted. He'd seen them in the magical world of the Realm. And in the Realm he'd fallen in love with Jessica, a beautiful fairy princess with golden red hair.

Princess Jessica had been born to be the Realm's true queen. But she'd run away with Robert to the mortal world, to Blue Moon, to become his wife.

More than fifty years had passed since then.

The blue dress Granny had worn on the night she'd left the Realm had faded to soft gray in the carved chest in her bedroom. Her golden red hair had turned white. But her eyes were still as green as they had ever been, and her smile was just as sweet.

Granny rarely returned to the Realm. She said that going back too often was unfair to her sister, Helena, who now ruled the Realm in her place. She said she was content with the life, and the world, she'd chosen. But when Jessie had shown her the party invitation on the day it arrived, she'd sighed.

"Lirralee," she'd said softly. "Oh, I used to go there often, with Patrice, long ago. It's in the hills, beside the stream that runs down to the Finding Pool."

"The Finding Pool? What's that?" Jessie had asked, fascinated.

"The most beautiful place. You'll see," Granny had smiled, her eyes filled with memories. "It was there that your grandfather and I met for the first time. Afterward, we visited it together often. Oh,

I'd love to see it again! I haven't seen the Finding Pool since the night we left the Realm."

"Then come with me to the party, Granny," Jessie had urged. "You can visit the Finding Pool again, on the way. And everyone in Lirralee will be so pleased to see you."

But Granny had shaken her head. "Just send them my love," she'd said. "And when you get back, tell me all about it."

Jessie reached the hedge and hurried into the place she called the secret garden. The warm air was filled with the scent of the rosemary bushes that surrounded the little square of smooth, green grass.

"Open!" Jessie whispered, and closed her eyes. She felt the cool, tingling breeze surround her as the invisible Door opened, and she was swept into the Realm.

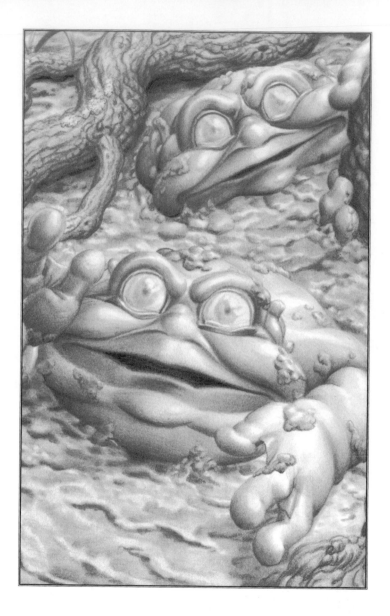

CHAPTER TWO

The Daisy Trail

Jessie opened her eyes. She was standing on the pebbly road on the Realm side of the Door. The sunshine was warm, and the air was filled with magic.

She could hear flower fairies chattering and laughing somewhere near. She would have loved to call to them, but she knew she couldn't. They'd want her to dance with them, and she didn't have time. By now it must be after two-thirty. She was very late.

She wasn't really dressed for running, but she had no choice. Her long skirt tangled around her ankles as she pounded along the road. She reached the familiar grove of pale-leafed trees and hurried through it, her party shoes slipping and sliding on the grass.

At last, the golden palace rose before her. The great front doors stood wide open, but Jessie ignored them. Panting, she hurried down the side of the palace, to the place where Patrice had her own little apartment.

Patrice's door was shut. Pinned to it was a bright yellow daisy, and a note.

Dear Jessie,
Sorry, but we couldn't wait any longer. We've got
a lot of the party food, so can't be late. Lirralee's
not far. Follow the daisy trail.
P, M, & G

"Oh, no!" Jessie groaned. "The daisy trail? But where's the daisy trail?"

She turned away from the door and looked miserably around her. Then, suddenly, she saw a spot of yellow on the ground. It was a yellow daisy, like the one fixed to the door. And there, not far beyond it, was another daisy, and another!

A trail of daisies led toward the back of the palace. Jessie laughed aloud. So *that* was what the note meant. Patrice, Giff, and Maybelle were dropping daisies as they walked, to show her the way!

She began to follow the daisy trail, picking up the little yellow flowers as she went. She had at least a dozen in her hand by the time the trail curved off to the right, and led into a thick wood.

The wood was dim and silent. Dark branches twisted together high above Jessie's head, making a leafy roof that blocked out the sun. The yellow daisies were harder to see now, and Jessie had to look carefully to find them. She walked on slowly, peering into the green shade ahead, her shoes sinking deep into a soft carpet of dead leaves.

The farther she went, the more uncomfortable she felt. It wasn't just the darkness and stillness of the wood. It was a feeling—a heavy feeling of sadness, loss, and anger—coming not from Jessie herself, but from somewhere else.

And then there came a moment when she couldn't see the next yellow daisy at all. The trail seemed to have ended, right in the middle of the wood.

She felt a little flutter of panic in her stomach. It looked as if someone — or something — had taken away the next part of the daisy trail. Now what would she do? With no daisies to guide her, she didn't dare go on. And . . . and she didn't dare turn back, either.

She looked behind her, biting her lip. She wished very much that she hadn't picked up the yellow daisies as she had reached them. It had seemed a good idea at the time. It was a shame to leave such pretty flowers on the ground to die.

But now there was nothing behind her to show where she had been. Her feet seemed to have left no trace in the leaves that covered the ground.

The silence of the wood seemed to close in around her. Her skin began to prickle. She felt as if she was being watched.

All will be well. That's what Granny always says, she told herself. *All will be well.*

But she didn't believe it. Her feeling of terror grew. She wanted to run — to run wildly away through the trees. She almost did it, too. But suddenly she thought of her mother. What would her mother say, if she were here?

Whatever happens, don't panic, Jessie. Keep your wits about you, and think.

Jessie imagined her mother's voice, calm and full of human common sense. She felt her panic die. She put one of the daisies from her bunch down at her feet, to mark the place where she had stopped. Then she walked forward a little way, looking carefully left and right.

And suddenly she saw the next daisy in the trail. It was behind the trunk of a huge tree, over to the right. No wonder she hadn't seen it from where she'd been standing before!

But now she could see it clearly. And she could see another daisy lying a little beyond it. Farther on, almost invisible in the dimness, there was yet another. The daisy trail hadn't stopped. It had just turned sharply to the right.

Jessie felt weak with relief. She turned right and began following the spots of yellow color once again.

The earth grew soft and damp beneath her feet. The trees began to thin. I must be getting close to the stream, she thought. Lirralee can't be far away now.

Her heart lifted at the thought that her journey had nearly ended. Clutching the little silver package and the bunch of daisies tightly, she began to hurry.

Soon there were no more trees. Jessie found herself dodging between huge clumps of dull green reeds that were as tall as she was. The ground grew wetter and stickier with every step. It squelched as she walked. Between the reed clumps, she could see the gleam of water not far ahead.

Then something caught her around the ankle. She stumbled. Her feet slid out from under her and, with a squeal, she sat down heavily in soft, squishy mud.

"Got her!" gurgled a harsh, bubbling voice.

There was a chorus of cheers, like the sound of water gurgling down a drain. Jessie looked around wildly. The mud by her left foot heaved, and she found herself looking at a small, fat, glistening brown creature with no neck, very short arms and legs, and pale, bulging eyes.

For an instant she thought it was a frog, then realized that it was something quite different. The creature's watery eyes were alive with mischief. Its wide, toothless mouth was stretched into a wicked grin.

"You tripped me!" Jessie shouted angrily.

The creature's mouth stretched wider. Its shapeless body began to shake. "Hurgle urgle urgle!" it spluttered. Jessie realized it was laughing.

Furious, she scrambled to her feet. Her shoes were covered in mud. Mud spattered her blue dress, the silver package, and the bunch of yellow daisies.

She opened her mouth to shout again, then felt herself sinking deeper into the mud. She looked down and saw more of the mud creatures gathered around her feet, pulling her shoes determinedly.

"Stop that!" she yelled. She dragged her feet free. They came out of the ooze with a horrible sucking sound. The creatures held on, clinging to her shoes in dripping brown clumps. Jessie kicked her feet in disgust. Gurgling with laughter, the creatures somersaulted backward into the mud and immediately began swimming toward her again.

And more of them were appearing every moment. There were dozens of them . . . hundreds!

The mud was heaving and bubbling. Everywhere Jessie looked there were bulging eyes, grinning mouths, and fat, rubbery fingers reaching for her.

"Why are you doing this?" she cried desperately. "What are you?"

"Mud wubbles, mud wubbles, mud wubbles," gurgled the creatures at her feet. "Hargle-argle-argle-argle! Hurgle-urgle-urgle-urgle!" Their gummy mouths stretched wide, and their glistening rolls of fat shook with laughter. They clapped their hands. Mud spattered everywhere.

"This way!" called a soft, clear voice.

Jessie looked around wildly and saw a pair of green eyes peering at her from behind a high clump of reeds. A delicate hand beckoned.

"You will be safe from the mud wubbles over here," the newcomer called. "Make haste!"

Jessie staggered toward the beckoning hand. She soon gave up trying to shake off the mud wubbles clinging to the hem of her dress and the soles of her shoes. It took all her concentration just to keep upright.

By the time she reached the clump of reeds, the green eyes and the beckoning hand had disappeared. But it didn't matter. Jessie had already seen what lay beyond the reeds.

It was a high bank, covered with fresh, green grass. Clear, shallow water—the edge of a shining lake—lapped at its base.

Gratefully, Jessie splashed through the shallow water and scrambled up the bank, out of the mud. As she climbed, dripping mud wubbles fell from her feet and skirt, groaning and complaining. By the time she reached the grass, she was free of them. The relief was tremendous!

She looked around for her helper. "Where are you?" she called. "Oh, please show yourself! I want to thank you!"

"I am here," said the soft voice. Startled, Jessie looked down. And there she saw, rising from the deeper water beyond the bank, a pale, pointed face, a pair of green eyes, and a cascade of pale green hair.

Jessie's heart thudded with excitement. She knew what she was seeing. This was a water sprite!

CHAPTER THREE

The finding pool

"I am Cool-of-the-Evening," said the water sprite gravely. "I am sorry the mud wubbles worried you with their tricks. They do not mean any real harm. They think it a great joke to make folk slip in the mud, that is all. I bid you welcome to the Finding Pool."

"The Finding Pool? But . . ." Jessie glanced quickly around, frowning in disappointment. Was *this* the place Granny had loved so much? The place she'd said was so beautiful?

Certainly, the high banks of this part of the pool were pretty, thickly covered with grass and flowers, and overhung by trees. They reminded Jessie of the banks of a pool in one of Robert Belairs's paintings: the water sprite picture called *Farewell* that hung in Granny's bedroom.

But the trees and flowers weren't reflected in deep, mirrorlike water as they were in the painting. Instead, they hung sadly over flat, glistening mud that was heaving with mud wubbles and dotted with clumps of stiff, dull-looking reeds. There was water only in the center of the pool and in a few deep spots like the place where Cool-of-the-Evening was standing.

Then Jessie's eyes fell on the bank of tall, bright green reeds that grew in the water at the pool's center. They looked very familiar, and her heart lurched.

This *was* the same pool as the one in the painting. But it was changed. Terribly changed.

"The mud around the edges of the pool used to be covered with water," she said aloud. "That's why the reeds there look so dull and sick. The pool is drying up."

She realized that Cool-of-the-Evening was

staring at her. "My name is Jessie," she said quickly. "Thank you so much for helping me. I don't know what I would have done if you hadn't. Those things—the mud wubbles—may not mean any harm, but there are so many of them!"

The water sprite nodded. "And there are more every day," she said. "Some have always lived here. But as the Finding Pool shrinks, more mud appears around its edges. And the more mud there is . . ." Her voice trailed off in a sigh.

"But why is the Finding Pool shrinking?" Jessie asked, leaning forward urgently. "Are the mud wubbles drinking up the water or something?"

Cool-of-the-Evening shook her head. "Mud wubbles do not like clear water," she said. "They drink only mud."

The surface of the pool rippled, and more water sprites appeared around her, their long, green hair floating like weeds in the water. Some were young and some were old, but all of them had skin as smooth as water lily petals and were dressed, like Cool-of-the-Evening, in trailing green. The children smiled at Jessie, but the adults merely bowed their heads in greeting and stood silent, their faces troubled.

The tallest of the other sprites turned his mysterious, water-colored eyes to Jessie. "The stream that flows down from the hills has somehow become blocked," he said. "Very little water now runs into the Finding Pool, but the hot sun still shines upon it. So the pool is slowly drying up."

"But—but surely you can clear the stream?" Jessie exclaimed. "If all of you worked together, it would be easy!"

All the sprites shook their heads. "We cannot intrude on the land above the Finding Pool, human child," said the tallest one calmly. "We cannot go upstream. This is an ancient law of the Realm, and we dare not break it."

Jessie shook her head impatiently. Sometimes the ways of the Realm seemed crazy to her. The sprites would rather see their home destroyed than break an old law that surely didn't matter any longer. Clearly a bit of human common sense was needed here, just as it had been needed in the wood.

She grabbed her silver-wrapped present and her flowers, and scrambled to her feet. "Well, there's no law that says *I* can't go upstream," she said briskly. "In fact, I'm going to a party in Lirralee right now. I'll clear the stream on my way. Just show me where it is."

A whispering sigh spread through the watching group. Jessie felt a warm glow. It was wonderful to think she could bring her new friends such relief.

The tallest sprite pointed to a mass of bushes and ferns at the far end of the pool. "The mouth of the stream is there," he said. "If you follow the dry bed, you will soon see where it is choked. And if indeed you can make the water flow again, you will earn the undying gratitude of the sprites of the Finding Pool."

"I'm happy to help," Jessie said. She grinned. "And it's the least I can do after Cool-of-the-Evening so kindly saved me from the mud wubbles."

The tallest sprite smiled back at her. But she saw that his eyes were still wary. He isn't sure I'll keep my promise, Jessie thought, with a stab of annoyance. *He thinks I might just go on to the party, and forget all about this place. Who does he think I am?*

"Perhaps," she said stiffly, "when the Finding Pool is filled again, I can come back, and visit you—like my grandmother Princess Jessica did long ago."

Her words had an even greater effect than she had expected. A shocked silence fell over the pool. The tallest sprite seemed to freeze. Cool-of-the-Evening raised her head, her eyes huge and startled.

"What is this?" hissed a dry old voice.

The sprites parted, like leaves blown over the surface of the water, as an old, bent sprite appeared among them.

"Birdwing," whispered Cool-of-the-Evening.

The old sprite called Birdwing raised his head. His eyes were dark and cold. "So—this child is the granddaughter of Queen Jessica, the true Queen of the Realm," he said. "What have you done, Bright-Light-on-Water?"

The tallest sprite stiffened, but turned to face his leader without flinching. "Are we to die before we seek help?" he demanded. "Whoever the girl is, she is strong enough to free the stream. And she is willing."

Jessie was suddenly very ashamed that she had spoken of her grandmother. She had only done it to make herself look important. And now proud old Birdwing seemed to think she was too important to help!

"There's nothing wrong with asking for help when you need it," she said. "And it doesn't matter who I am. It's just lucky I came along when I did."

Bright-Light-on-Water nodded, his face expressionless. Cool-of-the-Evening clasped her hands anxiously. Birdwing said nothing. He did not look convinced.

The only way to end this is to go and clear the stream, Jessie thought. Birdwing won't stay angry for long, once the pool begins to fill again.

"I must go," she said aloud. "Thanks again for helping me." She bowed awkwardly to Birdwing, nodded to Bright-Light-on-Water in what she hoped was a reassuring way, and smiled at Cool-of-the-Evening. Then she set off along the bank toward the cluster of bushes, reeds, and ferns that marked the mouth of the stream.

When she reached it, she looked back. The water sprites were still watching her. She raised her hand and waved. Bright-Light-on-Water and some of the smallest children waved back. None of the other sprites moved.

Jessie sighed and pushed through the bushes till she reached the streambed. It wound away from the pool like a deep, narrow path. Ferns grew thickly on both sides of it, but only a tiny trickle of water oozed over the smooth brown and white stones that lined its bed.

Jessie began to walk along beside it, watching the ground in case the mud wubbles came out of hiding again. Her clothes were almost dry now, but her shoes were still damp. At least the water washed most of the mud away, she thought. I won't look so bad when I get to the party. If I ever *do* get to the party, after all this.

And only then did she remember the daisy trail. She looked down at the daisies in her hand and frowned in puzzlement. She hadn't seen a yellow daisy on the ground since she blundered into the mud of the Finding Pool.

But before she could think about why that could be, she suddenly became aware of a new sound: the distant sound of running water, not far ahead.

She felt a small thrill of excitement, and began to walk faster. She rounded a bend and saw that just ahead the streambed passed through a narrow gap between two high rocks.

The gap was blocked by a thick tangle of sticks, leaves, and what looked like the remains of an old fishing net. Jessie could hear the babbling of a stream somewhere near, but only a little water trickled through the wall of rubbish that choked the gap in the rocks.

This was the place she'd been looking for.

jessie's good deed

When Jessie reached the blocked gap between the rocks, she saw that the land on the other side of the blockage was flooded. Unable to flow on, the stream had overflowed its banks, and the water had spread through a little valley that lay between the hills. Under the gleaming water Jessie could see drowned bushes, grass, and flowers. It was a mournful sight.

Across the flood she could see the upper part of the stream. Graceful trees with golden leaves lined its banks on both sides. She thought she could hear faint music in the distance, and guessed that the party at Lirralee had begun.

She felt a spark of anger. How could the people of Lirralee enjoy themselves while their stream was in this state? How could they be so careless?

She put down her silver package and her flowers. Holding on to one of the rocks, she leaned over the gap and began to pull at the mess that was choking the stream. She soon found that the net was the main problem. Somehow it had become twisted around both rocks, so that it stretched right across the gap. Sticks, leaves, and bits of bark had then become tangled in it as they were carried downstream.

She tugged furiously at the net. For a time it resisted all her efforts to free it. Then, suddenly, it tore loose. A lot of sticks and leaves came with it, but not all.

Jessie hauled the tangle of net onto the bank, then began digging at the mess still wedged between the rocks. She had only pulled away a few dripping handfuls, however, when she realized that the water was going to do the rest of her work for her.

Without the net to hold it in place, the mass of sticks, leaves, and bark could not resist the water. In moments it was breaking up. Soon water was flooding through the gap, carrying everything before it as it rushed eagerly downstream, gurgling and babbling over the stones.

Jessie sat back, brushing dirt and leaves from her hands. Well, that's one problem solved, anyway, she said to herself. She felt very pleased and satisfied. The freed water was running so fast that already it had filled the streambed as far as she could see. Soon it would reach the Finding Pool.

She imagined the shrieks of the water sprite children as cool water streamed into their pool. She imagined Cool-of-the-Evening smiling with joy and Bright-Light-on-Water raising his eyebrows as he realized that the human child really *had* kept her promise. She imagined the mud wubbles grumbling, flip-flopping away as the slimy mud disappeared beneath clear, sparkling water.

She wished she could see it for herself, and for a moment she was tempted to go back downstream, instead of moving on to the party. She still felt annoyed with the people of Lirralee. The stream had obviously been blocked for weeks—maybe even for months! The water sprites had been suffering for all that time—and the little valley had been flooded, too. Someone should have done something about it long ago.

Then she shrugged, picked up her silver package, and climbed to her feet. I said I'd go to the party, so I'll have to go, she thought. Patrice, Giff, and Maybelle will worry about me if I don't turn up.

She moved a little way downstream, climbed a small hill, and, keeping to the high ground, began trudging toward the double line of golden trees that marked the upper part of the stream. The darkness of the wood rose to her left, and to her right was the view of the flooded valley.

She could see that the floodwater was already beginning to go down. In an hour or two, no doubt, it would have shrunk back to the streambed, where it belonged. But she knew that the valley would take months to recover from its drenching.

It's just very lucky that someone with common sense came along to fix things, she told herself crossly.

When she reached the upper part of the stream at last, she saw that it was straighter and wider than the stream on the other side of the valley. The crystal clear water rippled and sang between banks of flowers, ferns, and mossy stones. The gold-leaved trees made a delicious, dappled shade, and violets carpeted the ground beneath them.

Jessie began walking along the stream, trying to tread softly on the violet carpet. Her heart grew lighter with every step. It was impossible to stay in a bad mood in such an enchanting place. Besides, the joyful music was louder now, and over the babbling of the water Jessie could hear the distant sound of chattering, laughing voices.

A little wooden bridge came into view. And . . . Jessie stared. On the ground in front of the bridge was a tiny spot of bright yellow. She ran forward. Sure enough, a yellow daisy lay on the carpet of violets. And other daisies lay on the bridge itself, and along the bank on the other side of the stream!

Jessie shook her head, smiling ruefully. She'd found the daisy trail again, just when she didn't really need it anymore! She glanced to her left and saw more yellow daisies, stretching in a long line out of the darkness of the wood.

Suddenly she felt rather foolish. The daisy trail probably led through the wood straight to the bridge. Patrice, Giff, and Maybelle had done their best to lead her to Lirralee by the shortest way possible. But all their trouble had been for nothing. First, the mud wubbles had driven the daisy trail from her mind, and then she'd got all mixed up in the water sprites' problems. So she'd come the long way, following the stream.

I'm glad I did it, though, she thought, turning to cross the bridge. I'm glad I met the water sprites and was able to help them, even if it did make me wet and muddy and late. And when I get to Lirralee I'll tell them they should look after things a bit better.

She reached the other side of the stream and began following the daisy trail along the stream. She saw a cluster of small red, blue, green, and yellow canoes drawn up on the bank not far ahead. Then she saw movement through the trees. She saw a clearing, bright colors, a big table, and small people dancing. Music, singing, and the sound of chattering, laughing voices floated to her ears. She found herself smiling.

"Jessie! Jessie!" One voice shrilled above all the rest. And suddenly Giff the elf was swinging down from the branch of a tree beside the clearing and bounding toward her. A chain of yellow daisies decorated Giff's cap. His face was split in a wide grin.

"Jessie's here!" he shouted over his shoulder. "Jessie's here! Hooray!"

A chorus of answering cheers rose from the clearing. Patrice came running, surrounded by a group of small, plump people who looked exactly like her. All of them were waving, smiling, and shouting words of welcome.

Jessie waved back. And all at once she decided not to say anything about the choked stream, or the flood, or the Finding Pool—not today, anyway. Everyone looked so happy, and so pleased to see her. She didn't want to spoil things by scolding them.

I'll say something to Patrice tomorrow, Jessie thought. I've fixed the problem for now. In a day or two, Patrice can quietly tell her family what happened, and ask them to make sure the stream never gets blocked again.

Then she didn't have time to think any more, because Giff threw himself into her arms with a shout of joy, nearly knocking her flat. The next moment, Patrice had seized her arm, and a chattering, happy crowd was surrounding her, and sweeping her on to the party.

Maybelle the miniature horse was waiting in the clearing. She was all dressed up for the party. Her hooves shone with gold dust, and her white mane was threaded with green ribbons and tiny golden bells. Jessie stumbled up to her, laughing and out of breath, with Patrice holding tightly to her arm and Giff still hanging around her neck.

"At last!" Maybelle snapped, pawing the ground and tossing her head so that the little bells jingled. "Where in the Realm have you been,

Jessie? We're all starving, and they wouldn't start the Welcome without you."

"I—um—I'm really sorry," Jessie panted. "Something at home kept me late and then—"

"Oh, take no notice of Maybelle, dearie!" Patrice laughed, prizing Giff's arms from around Jessie's neck and swinging him firmly to one side. "She's just dying to get her nose into the sugar bowl, that's all. You're here now, and that's all that matters. Come and meet baby Jewel."

She, Giff, and Maybelle led Jessie to a large tree beside the stream. A happy-looking couple sat beneath the tree's spreading branches, surrounded by piles of gifts. Between them stood a wooden cradle decorated with garlands of flowers.

"This is my youngest niece, Lily, and her husband, Gem," said Patrice. "And this is their precious Jewel."

Jessie sank to her knees beside the cradle. Inside, kicking and cooing on a blanket of soft moss, lay the smallest, sweetest baby she had ever seen.

CHAPTER FIVE

The party by the stream

Jewel was no bigger than Jessie's hand, and was dressed in a red cap, a yellow smock, and bright red leggings. Nut brown curls peeped out from under her cap, her black eyes twinkled, and her mouth was like a pink rosebud.

"Hello, Jewel," Jessie whispered. She held out her little finger. Jewel opened her eyes wide, gurgled with delight, and grabbed the fingertip with both chubby hands.

Jessie's heart melted.

"Isn't she so *cute*?" squealed Giff, bending over the cradle and tickling Jewel under the chin. "Say hello to your uncle Giffie-Wiffie, Jewel. Give Uncle Giffie-Wiffie a smile. Oh, cutie-wootie-boo-boo-boo!"

"Pull yourself together, you fool of an elf!" muttered Maybelle. But Jessie saw her shake her bells at Jewel to make her smile when she thought no one was looking.

"She's beautiful!" Jessie exclaimed. "She's the most beautiful baby ever!"

Lily and Gem beamed. "We wished for her so long," Lily said. "I must admit, I'd almost given up hope we'd ever have a child. But Gem always said that our luck would change—and it did. Here's our little treasure at last."

"Queen Helena and Princess Christie sent her a gold bracelet," Gem put in proudly. "They would have come to the Welcome Party, too, if they hadn't had to go to Hidden Valley for the fairy-apple festival."

Maybelle snorted disapprovingly.

"They'd told the gnomes they'd go, and they couldn't break their promise, could they?" said Patrice briskly. "Anyway, now that you're here,

Jessie, the Welcome ceremony can begin. I'll gather everyone together."

As Patrice trotted away, Giff nudged Jessie in the ribs. "Is that a present for Jewel, Jessie?" he asked in a piercing whisper, jerking his head at the silver package still clutched in Jessie's hand.

"Oh, of course!" Jessie exclaimed. "I'd forgotten!" She gently eased her finger away from Jewel, and handed the package to Lily, wishing it weren't so crumpled and smeared with mud. "I'm sorry it's a bit messy," she said awkwardly. "I—I dropped it on my way here."

She watched nervously as Lily and Gem opened the silver wrapping. She'd made Jewel a soft toy fish out of a scrap of blue and white spotted material that Granny had given her.

She'd worked hard on the little fish. She'd had fun embroidering its eyes and its gills and its smile. She'd felt proud of it as she'd wrapped it up. But now, looking around at all the other gifts—carved wooden toys, pretty bonnets, gaily striped rugs, painted cups and bowls, and the gold bracelet sent by Queen Helena—she was afraid her present would seem too small and simple.

She needn't have worried. When they saw the little fish, Lily and Gem both exclaimed in admiration and pleasure. And when they held it out to Jewel, the baby stretched out her chubby hands and clutched it, gurgling happily.

All through the speeches and songs of the Welcome ceremony, Jewel held tightly to the blue-spotted fish. She chuckled at it, babbled to it, and sometimes sucked it, as if to see if it tasted as good as it looked. She wouldn't give it up, even when she was handed around to receive a kiss from everyone in the village. And when at last the ceremony was over, and she was put back in her basket, she yawned and went peacefully to sleep with Fishy cuddled in her arms.

Lily and Gem hung the cradle from a branch stretching low over the stream, so that Jewel would be soothed by the rippling sound of water as she slept. Then they packed up all the gifts in a big bundle. And then the music started up again, and the party really began.

For the next two hours, Jessie had the most

wonderful time. She met all Patrice's brothers, sisters, nieces, nephews, cousins, second cousins, and friends. She ate honey cookies, rainbow jellies, sugar cakes shaped like flowers, and many other good things. She drank sparkling pink berry juice poured from stone bottles kept deliciously cool in the stream. She danced beneath the trees, whirling in giddy circles, holding tightly to the small, brown hands of the people on either side of her. She joined in all the games.

Finally, she flopped on the ground beside Maybelle, who was resting in the shade and looking very content.

"What a wonderful party!" Jessie sighed.

"It's not bad," said Maybelle, licking a few stray grains of sugar from her lips. She raised her head, and the little bells jingled merrily as her mane was tossed by the breeze. "Look at that fool of an elf," she said, watching Giff capering madly in the middle of a circle of Patrice's cousins. "He'll be exhausted by the end of this. Well, if he thinks I'm going to carry him home, he can think again."

Jessie laughed. Lazily she turned her own face

up to the breeze. Above her head, leaves fluttered and branches swayed. "It's much windier than it was," she said. "I hadn't noticed."

Then something made her look toward the stream—to the branch where Jewel's cradle hung.

And the cradle was gone. The ribbon that had fastened it to the branch was flapping freely in the breeze.

Jessie's stomach turned over. With a cry she jumped to her feet.

"What is it?" Maybelle yawned.

Jessie could hardly speak. "Maybelle!" she choked. "The baby—Jewel—"

Maybelle looked over to where the cradle had hung and yawned again. "Oh yes, I see," she said lazily. "The wind must have undone the ribbon. They should have tied it more tightly. I thought so at the time."

"*Maybelle!*" screamed Jessie. "The baby's in the water! Oh—"

Frantically she ran to the stream, shouting for help. The music faltered and died. The people stopped dancing and stared. Then all of them came running, Patrice, Giff, Lily, and Gem at the head of the crowd.

"The cradle fell into the stream!" Jessie heard herself screaming in horror. "Oh, the baby, the baby . . ."

To her astonishment, everyone began to laugh. Patrice patted her arm. "Don't worry, dearie," Patrice said. "A little sail along the stream won't do Jewel any harm. In fact, she'll love it, if she's awake. Her cradle is made for sailing. That's how it's done in Lirralee."

"But what if the cradle tips over?" cried Jessie.

"It won't," said Gem, looking quite offended. "I made it myself, and it's as steady a little boat as you'll ever see. Jewel's sailed downstream in it lots of times, with never a problem."

"And if it does catch on a rock and tip up this time, then what of it?" chirped Lily. "Jewel loves swimming!"

Astounded, still shaking with shock and fear, Jessie looked wildly at Patrice.

"Our babies aren't like human babies, Jessie," said Patrice gently. "They can swim like fish from

49

the moment they're born. They spend more time in the water than out of it. Jewel's quite safe in the stream."

"All the same, someone had better run and fetch her," rumbled Patrice's oldest uncle, a very stout old man with nut brown eyebrows and a long white beard. "The birds have begun going to their nests. The Welcome party is nearly over, but it would not be proper for our guests to leave without saying goodbye to Jewel."

"Pip and Bubbles have already gone to get her, Uncle Bon," squeaked one of the second cousins. "They ran downstream as soon as Princess Jessie called the alarm."

"Very good," rumbled Uncle Bon. Courteously, he bowed to Jessie. "I am sorry you were frightened," he said. "But I am surprised. Has your dear grandmother never told you of Lirralee and its ways?"

But before Jessie could answer, there were shrieks from the trees beyond the village. The next moment, two curly-headed figures were tumbling into the clearing and rushing, panting, to the crowd beside the stream.

Jessie's heart jolted as she recognized the twins, Pip and Bubbles. A little while ago she had played a chasing game with them. Then they had been laughing. Now their chubby, identical faces were twisted with fear.

Lily gave a small cry and pressed her hand to her mouth.

"What's happened, Pip?" barked Gem, putting his arm around his wife.

"Our dam, Gem!" One of the twins gasped. "Someone—some enemy—has broken down our dam! The net we fastened across the stream has been torn away!"

Jessie's stomach turned over. She felt her face burning.

"The stream is running again, as fast as ever." The other twin gasped. "And there's no sign of Jewel. We think—we think—that she must have been swept all the way to the Finding Pool."

And suddenly the clearing was ringing with cries of fear and horror.

Patrice, her hands clasped tightly together, was talking rapidly to Uncle Bon. They both glanced at Jessie, and she felt her face grow even hotter.

Did they suspect that it was she who had broken down the dam, and pulled away the net?

But why should it matter so much anyway? she thought desperately. The Finding Pool's not so far away. They can just go downstream and—

Uncle Bon cleared his throat and held up his arms. "Folk of Lirralee!" he boomed.

Silence fell at once. Frightened faces turned toward him.

"Lily and Gem, do not fear!" Uncle Bon said. "We will go to the Finding Pool. We will make the sprites listen to us."

"They have never listened before," said Gem in a low, harsh voice, and everyone murmured in agreement.

"This time it will be different," Uncle Bon said firmly. "This time, as Patrice has pointed out, Princess Jessie will be with us. Jessie is our true queen's granddaughter. The water sprites will not dare to defy her!"

Everyone looked at Jessie, who nodded uncertainly. She felt frightened, and completely bewildered. What was going on?

CHAPTER SIX

The Tale
of the Moon Stone

"Let us go!" cried Lily. "Oh, quickly, quickly!" She ran to the stream and began pulling at the rope that fastened a blue canoe to a tree trunk. The crowd surged after her, making for the other canoes.

"Stop!" Uncle Bon roared. "If we are to succeed, this must not look like an invasion! Only a very small group can go."

"Lily and I will not stay behind," growled Gem, striding to Lily's side and looking at Uncle Bon defiantly. "Jewel is our child, and it is our right—"

"Of course." Uncle Bon sighed. "I would not be

so foolish as to try to stop you, Gem. I will go with you and Lily in *Dragonfly*. Patrice and Jessie can take my boat. Everyone else must stay here."

Ignoring the crowd's groans of protest, he strode to the stream, beckoning Jessie and Patrice to follow him. Rapidly he untied a green canoe called *The Frog*.

"Go with speed, Patrice," he muttered as Jessie scrambled into the canoe and took the end seat. "I will do everything I can to delay Gem and Lily. I will take my time getting into *Dragonfly*, and my weight will slow it once we are underway. With luck, you will get to the Finding Pool long before us. Gem is a good-hearted boy, but too often he acts without thinking. I fear he might lose his temper with the sprites and spoil our chances."

Patrice nodded agreement. She took her place on the center seat of *The Frog*, and grabbed the paddle. With a grunt, Uncle Bon pushed the canoe into the middle of the stream. The next moment, the swift-flowing current had caught it, and it was speeding downstream.

Feeling as if she were in a dream, Jessie watched Patrice's sturdy back as the palace housekeeper expertly steered the frail craft down the center of the stream. Then she became aware of faint shouts behind her. She twisted in her seat to look back.

Lirralee was rapidly slipping away into the distance. The bank of the stream was thronged with people. Among them Jessie could see the white figure of Maybelle, her mane and tail fluttering in the wind as she peered after the boat. And there was Giff, leaning precariously over the stream, waving frantically.

"Is *Dragonfly* coming after us yet?" asked Patrice.

"Not yet," Jessie answered.

"Good," said Patrice. "We need every moment we can get alone with the sprites."

"Patrice—Patrice, I don't understand what's happening!" Jessie wailed. "Surely the water sprites won't hurt Jewel? They couldn't be so cruel! Granny loved them. Grandpa, too. They—"

"This is the problem, Jessie," said Patrice, paddling furiously as if to relieve her feelings. "Ancient Realm law forbids the people of Lirralee and the water sprites of the Finding Pool from entering one another's territories without being invited. Officially, the people of Lirralee own what is in the stream, and the water sprites own whatever comes to the Finding Pool."

"But—" Jessie's heart was pounding. "But what if something really *important* falls into the stream and is swept down to the Finding Pool? Surely—"

"Until just lately, the water sprites were not unreasonable," said Patrice. "If anything important was swept down to the Finding Pool, they would play a special tune on a flute they called the Finding Flute. That was an invitation to the people of Lirralee to come and fetch whatever it was that had been lost. But all that's changed now."

"W—why?" Jessie stammered. "What changed it?"

Patrice sighed, her eyes fixed on the stream ahead. "The trouble started about a year ago," she said. "There was a lot of magic in the air then, and everyone in the Realm was a bit—well, a bit overexcited, if you know what I mean."

"I remember," Jessie said. "Queen Helena's griffins went strange, and I had to come to the Realm to calm them down."

"So you did." Patrice nodded. "Well, for a few days, life in Lirralee was one big party. And, what with the dancing and playing around and all, a lot of things ended up falling into the stream and being carried down to the Finding Pool. Chairs and balls and coats and teapots and—oh, all sorts of things. After a while, the water sprites played the Finding Flute. The whole of Lirralee went downstream—still in a party mood, of course, because of the magic."

She broke off and expertly steered the canoe around a rock. "It's a good thing I still remember how to paddle one of these things," she muttered.

"Patrice! Go on!" Jessie begged.

"Well, I didn't hear about all this till the next day, because I was at the palace," said Patrice. "But apparently, after the Lirralee people had got their things back, and were just about to leave the Finding Pool, the water sprites discovered that their Moon Stone had disappeared."

"The Moon Stone?" Jessie exclaimed. "What's that, Patrice? Granny's never told me about—"

"Jessica wouldn't know of it," Patrice broke in. "It was found in the Finding Pool the morning after she left the Realm, to live in your world, at the time of the blue moon before last. It became the sprites' greatest treasure. They believed it was the moon's gift to them and would bring them good fortune. It's a pale blue stone, round, gleaming, and very smooth to touch, like a big blue pearl, or a tiny blue moon."

A picture leaped into Jessie's mind—a picture so clear that it was almost like a memory. It was as if she'd actually seen the Moon Stone, and held it in her hand.

"So—the water sprites had the Moon Stone for over fifty years?" she said. "And a year ago it was lost?"

Patrice nodded. "The sprites were convinced that one of the Lirralee people had stolen it. But everyone denied knowing anything about it at all."

"So the sprites got angry," Jessie said dully. She felt sick, but she knew it wasn't because of the rocking of the canoe. It was because she knew how this story was going to end.

"The sprites were furious," Patrice agreed. "They said that until their treasure was returned to them, they would no longer return anything that drifted into the Finding Pool from Lirralee."

She sighed heavily. "And so it has been ever since. The sprites return nothing that comes to them—nothing, however valuable or important it is. That's why the Lirralee people finally put a net across the stream—to catch things before they swept too far . . . and were lost to them forever."

Frozen with horror, Jessie saw that the canoe was about to enter the drowned valley. They had almost reached the place where she'd pulled away the net—the net that would have saved Jewel, if it had still been in place. I'll have to tell Patrice what I did, she thought. But she couldn't find the words.

"There's been a flood here," Patrice said, looking quickly from side to side at the valley's sodden earth and the broad puddles of water that still lay here and there. "The net must have got clogged with bark and leaves, so the stream flooded the valley.

How could Uncle Bon have let that happen?"

"Pip told Gem that their 'dam' had been broken down," said Jessie in a low voice. "It sounded to me as if he, Bubbles, and Gem knew that the stream was blocked, even if Uncle Bon didn't."

"You're right!" Patrice gasped. "Oh, those naughty, troublemaking boys! How could they—?"

Her voice broke off as she steered the canoe through the gap in the rocks. Jessie saw her glance at the bank. A great heap of damp sticks, bark, leaves, and twisted netting lay where Jessie had left them. And Jessie's cheeks flamed as she saw, lying beside the heap, a small bunch of wilted yellow daisies.

Patrice's shoulders stiffened. She looked quickly over her shoulder, and met Jessie's eyes.

Jessie wet her lips, and nodded. "Yes," she said in a small voice. "I was here. And I unblocked the stream."

Patrice's eyes widened in shock. She turned back to her paddling without a word.

Jessie's throat tightened. "I didn't know that the net had been put there for a reason, Patrice!"

she burst out. "I thought it had just floated down-stream and got caught between the rocks, with all the other stuff. The water sprites didn't tell me—"

"The water sprites?" snapped Patrice. "But when did you see the water sprites, Jessie? The daisy trail didn't go near the Finding Pool."

"Yes, it did!" Jessie exclaimed. "It led right into it—or at least, into the mud at the edge—in that place where there are no high banks. These awful things called mud wubbles were all around me, and—"

"What?" Patrice gasped. "But, Jessie, the daisy trail went straight through the forest to the Lirralee bridge. That's by far the quickest way. Someone must have moved the daisies on purpose to lead you astray."

Jessie nodded dismally, suddenly realizing who that someone had been. She remembered a tall, silent figure with watchful, water-colored eyes. She remembered old Birdwing hissing in anger . . . *this child is the granddaughter of Queen Jessica, the true Queen of the Realm. What have you done, Bright-Light-on-Water?*

CHAPTER SEVEN

THE BARGAIN

"I think it was one of the water sprites," Jessie said slowly. "I think he overheard you, Giff, and Maybelle talking as you walked through the forest. He saw you laying the daisy trail. He realized that a human child would be coming along, very soon. So he moved the daisies, to lead me to the Finding Pool—"

"Bright-Light-on-Water!" Patrice muttered.

"I think so," said Jessie. "But how did you know?"

"It wasn't hard to guess." Patrice shrugged. "I've known Bright-Light-on-Water since he was a child. He's clever, and daring, and very restless. He and Gem are two of a kind, in a way. After the Moon Stone disappeared, he wanted to invade Lirralee and search all the houses till it was found. Birdwing, the sprites' leader, put a stop to that plan, but I hear that some of the sprites still think Bright-Light-on-Water was right."

"He arranged for another sprite—one called Cool-of-the-Evening—to save me from the mud wubbles," Jessie said. "I realize now that it was so that I'd feel grateful to the sprites and want to help them. He told me the stream was blocked, and of course I offered to clear it. But he didn't say a word about the net. I didn't know. . . ." She swallowed desperately, fighting back her tears.

"The cunning, wicked creature!" Patrice exploded. "How dare he trick you like that! You, the granddaughter of the true queen!"

"He didn't know who I was," Jessie said. "None of them did at first. And the Finding Pool was drying up, Patrice. No water was flowing into it at all. Bright-Light-on-Water must have been desperate to save it."

"Perhaps," Patrice said grimly. "But if it had been only that, he'd have told you about the net. He *wanted* the net removed. He wanted something like this to happen. He— Oh!" Her voice broke off in a high squeak. "Oh, we've come too far!"

The canoe had rounded a bend, and there, not far ahead, was the Finding Pool, gleaming in the last rays of the sun. Patrice paddled madly, vainly trying to turn the nose of the canoe toward the bank. "Jessie, catch hold of something!" she squealed. "Stop us!"

Jessie leaned over the edge of the canoe and grabbed a branch hanging over the water. For a terrible moment she thought she was going to be pulled right out of the canoe, but she curled her legs under her seat and held on grimly.

The canoe came to a stop. Breathing hard, Patrice dug the paddle into the rushing water and at last managed to pull the canoe out of the center of the stream and into the reeds clustered at the bank.

"Don't let go, Jessie," she warned. Nimbly she jumped out of the canoe, pulled it farther up the bank, and tied it firmly to a rock. "All right," she said, straightening up and fanning herself. "You can let go now and get out."

Gingerly, Jessie scrambled onto the bank. The reeds tickled her face and arms. The soggy ground squelched beneath her feet. She looked down quickly, but couldn't see any mud wubbles. That doesn't mean they're not there, though, she thought. I'll have to be careful.

"Oh, that was a near thing, Jessie!" Patrice panted. "One more minute and we'd have been in the pool ourselves!"

"Then we would have had two more prisoners," said a cool voice. "That would have been amusing."

Jessie and Patrice spun around. There, staring at them through the reeds, was Bright-Light-on-Water. Several more sprites were gathered behind him. Cool-of-the-Evening was among them. She and the others looked anxious, but Bright-Light-on-Water's head was held high, and his eyes were as dark and cold as a puddle on a cloudy winter's day.

"Greetings, Patrice of Lirralee," he said, bowing in a mocking way. "It is long since we saw you at the Finding Pool."

"Greetings, Bright-Light-on-Water," Patrice said evenly. "I believe you have already met Princess Jessie. She and I have come to see Birdwing. Please tell him we are here."

"Birdwing is resting," said Bright-Light-on-Water. "He is very old and frail these days—far too old to be troubled by small matters. Would you care to speak to me in his place?"

"No, I would not!" Patrice snapped. She looked over his shoulder to where Cool-of-the-Evening and the other sprites hovered uncertainly. "We must speak to Birdwing himself," she said in a louder voice. "If you value the peace of the Realm, you will tell him so at once."

Bright-Light-on-Water's eyes narrowed. "That sounds like a threat, Patrice," he said. "I advise you to watch your tongue."

"Oh, do you?" cried Patrice, suddenly losing her temper. "Well, I advise you to do as I say!"

The tall sprite smiled thinly. "You see how these Lirralee people speak to us?" he murmured to the sprites behind him. "They think they can steal from us, and dam the stream to dry up the

Finding Pool, without fear. They think we are weak, and no wonder, for until today we have acted with weakness. But no more."

"Oh, please!" said Jessie, unable to keep silent any longer. "Please give Jewel back to us. You have no quarrel with her. She's just a little baby! She needs her mother and father, just like your children need you!"

Bright-Light-on-Water straightened his shoulders. "Of course," he said politely. "And I can well understand your feelings, Princess Jessie. You were kind enough to clear the stream and, as a result, the child was swept into our hands. Her loss was your fault. Naturally you want to get her back. And, fortunately, there is a simple way for you to do it."

Jessie's heart leaped. "What is it?" she exclaimed. "I'll do anything!"

The sprite's smile broadened. "Unmask the Lirralee thief, Jessie," he said softly. "Find the Moon Stone. Return it to us. Then we will give you the child."

"But how can *I* find the thief?" Jessie cried.

"And how do you know there *is* a thief, anyway? For all you know, the Moon Stone is just lost in the pool somewhere!"

"Do you think we have not thought of that?" said Bright-Light-on-Water scornfully. "We have searched the pool floor, the reeds, and the banks a hundred times. The Moon Stone is not here."

There was a thump and some shouts from a little farther along the stream. Jessie glanced at Patrice, who made a despairing face.

"Patrice!" roared a voice Jessie recognized as Gem's. "Where are you? Have you found Jewel? Watch out, Lily! Ah—curse these mud wubbles! Get away, you brutes! Get away!"

"Ah," said Bright-Light-on-Water. "We have more visitors, it seems. The baby's parents, per-haps?"

"Yes," said Patrice shortly. "And if you will not return the child, I beg that you will at least fetch Birdwing. He should be here to deal with this."

"I have told you!" snarled Bright-Light-on-Water. "Birdwing is not to be disturbed. He is far too—"

"Far too *what*?" The old voice was strong, and filled with anger. Bright-Light-on-Water grew very still. Then, slowly, he turned.

Birdwing emerged from the reeds behind him, leaning on Cool-of-the-Evening's arm. "I am sorry," Cool-of-the-Evening said softly, flinching as she met Bright-Light-on-Water's furious eyes. "But Patrice is right. We need Birdwing's wisdom to guide us here."

"Indeed?" said Bright-Light-on-Water coldly. "And will Birdwing, in his wisdom, bow once again to the bullies of Lirralee? Will he destroy our only chance of having the Moon Stone returned to us?"

"Gem! Lily!" bellowed the distant voice of Uncle Bon before Birdwing could answer. "Wait! I'm stuck in this mud! Oh, lawks! Stop it, mud wubbles! Lily and Gem, wait for me!"

Clearly, his companions were taking no notice. Running feet were crashing through the reeds. And all of a sudden Gem and Lily were upon them, red-faced and panting. Giggling mud wubbles clung to their shoes, to Gem's trousers, and to the hem of Lily's skirt, but Lily and Gem didn't care. Ignoring Patrice, Jessie, and Bright-Light-on-Water, they threw themselves at Birdwing.

"Return our child, Birdwing!" Gem shouted, seizing the old sprite's shoulders. "Give her back, or it will be the worse for you!"

The other sprites leaped forward angrily, but Birdwing raised his hand to stop them. Jessie watched in dismay as his gentle eyes hardened, and his mouth formed a grim, straight line. "I have been accused of being too soft with your people, man of Lirralee," he said harshly. "Your threats show me that this is true. Hear this! The law is on our side. You will have your child when we have our Moon Stone. That is all I have to say."

He slipped from Gem's grasp as easily as water slips through a closed fist. And in a blink, he had melted into the reeds, and was gone.

The shadows seemed to flicker. In terror, Jessie looked around her. She, Patrice, Gem, and Lily were completely surrounded by silent water sprites. Every one of them, even Cool-of-the-Evening, was holding a gleaming crystal dagger.

CHAPTER EIGHT

A DiscoverY

"You would do well to leave here now, people of Lirralee," said Bright-Light-on-Water, his voice like ice.

"Not without Jewel!" cried Lily. "Oh, she is so small! She will be hungry! She will be afraid! I beg you—"

"Your infant is well," said Cool-of-the-Evening softly. "She has been fed and is sweetly sleeping. We know how to care for little ones. Do not fear for her."

"Only fear that you will never see her again," snapped Bright-Light-on-Water. "For that is how it will be, unless you surrender the Moon Stone."

Gem drew himself up. "Then, as no one in Lirralee has your wretched Moon Stone, sprite," he spat, "you had better prepare for war! We will go back to Lirralee now. But we will return, and when we do, we will not be alone."

He put his arm around the sobbing Lily. Together they turned, and hurried away.

Bright-Light-on-Water turned to the other sprites. His eyes were gleaming. "Spread the word that there is to be an attack," he said. "The people of Lirralee are showing their true colors at last. We must rouse ourselves to fight!"

"No!" Jessie cried. But the sprites paid her no attention at all.

She felt a small, rough hand grasp hers. "Jessie, come with me!" Patrice whispered urgently. She darted through the reeds and into the trees beyond, dragging Jessie with her.

"Where are we going?" Jessie panted as they threaded their way through the darkening forest.

"I'm going to the palace, to send a message to Queen Helena," panted Patrice. "Then I'm coming straight back with some guards, to try to keep the peace. You're going to fetch your grandmother. The sprites might listen to her. Oh, this is terrible! Terrible!"

And it's all my fault! thought Jessie. There's going to be war in the Realm. And it's all my fault!

Home at last, Jessie took the back steps two at a time and hurled herself through the back door. The kitchen was empty, but two places were set at the table, and something in the oven smelled good. She could hear her mother's clear, sensible voice floating from the front door.

"If you take my advice, Louise, you'll try to remember exactly what you did this morning, from the moment you woke up till the moment you found the ring missing. Act it out. That's the best way to find things you've lost."

As Mrs. Tweedie murmured in reply, Jessie slipped into the hallway and ran on tiptoe to her grandmother's bedroom. She thought that Granny might be there, keeping out of Mrs. Tweedie's way. But only Flynn was in Granny's room, snoozing in the center of the bed. He opened his golden eyes and blinked at Jessie lazily.

"Louise, I really wouldn't go around saying things like that," Jessie heard Rosemary say, a little more firmly. "It's far more likely that the ring has been lost than that Mr. Wiseman has stolen it. Why don't I come around after dinner and help you look?"

There was another fretful murmur from Mrs. Tweedie.

"It's no trouble at all," Rosemary said. "I'm sure Mum would have been pleased to come, too, but she won't be back till tomorrow. She and her friend Hazel suddenly decided to go down to the city, to some all-night movie festival. They've got more energy than I have, I can tell you!"

Jessie's heart sank to the soles of her shoes. "Oh, Flynn," she wailed softly. "I can't believe that Granny's away, tonight of all nights! By the time she gets back it'll be too late. The Lirralee people and the water sprites will be fighting for sure!"

Flynn's eyes widened. He turned his head to look at the painting of the Finding Pool, which hung opposite the door, above Granny's carved wooden chest.

"Yes," said Jessie. "It seems impossible, doesn't

it? It looks so peaceful. But it wasn't very peaceful this afternoon. And soon it'll be much, much worse! The only way to stop the fighting now is to get the Moon Stone back. But how can I do that?"

Flynn purred. The tip of his tail twitched. Blinking away hot tears, Jessie switched on the bedroom light and moved toward the water sprite painting. She'd known it all her life, and she'd always loved it. Now she looked at it with new eyes.

The scene was early evening, but Robert Belairs had painted a blue moon in the sky, so that the Finding Pool was bathed in the moon's soft, mysterious light. The sky was soft gray, and the air was filled with flecks of gold, shimmering with magic.

Sprites of every age were laughing and playing in the moonlit water of the Finding Pool. A few young ones were climbing up the banks, waving to an old sprite standing alone beside a large treasure chest in the reeds at the pool's center. Guessing this was why the painting was called *Farewell*, Jessie had once asked her grandmother where the young sprites were going. Granny had only shrugged and smiled. Usually she liked discussing her husband's paintings, but she always seemed to avoid talking about this one. It was as if it was too special, too private, for words.

Jessie looked carefully at the treasure chest, trying to find the Moon Stone. Then she realized that, of course, it wouldn't be there. Her grandfather had never seen it. It hadn't appeared in the Finding Pool till the morning after he and Granny had left the Realm.

She turned her gaze to the red-haired fairy princess sitting at the edge of the pool. That was Granny—Princess Jessica of the Realm, as she had been in those days. Jessica's long, golden red hair was held back by a simple silver band. Her gown was palest blue, tied at the waist with a plaited silver cord. She was playing dreamily with the ends of the cord, smiling as she looked out over the water.

There seems to be something a little bit sad about that smile, Jessie thought. I've never noticed that before.

Then she saw something else she hadn't noticed before. On the grass beside the princess was a smudge of shimmering gray. Jessie peered at it and suddenly realized what it was.

"That's Granny's cloak of invisibility, Flynn," she murmured. "How strange! Why would she have had that with her at the Finding Pool?"

And all at once she remembered something her grandmother had said that very afternoon.

I haven't seen the Finding Pool since the night we left the Realm . . . since the night we left the Realm. . . .

Suddenly everything fell into place. Suddenly Jessie knew that her grandfather hadn't just added the blue moon and the flecks of gold to the scene to give it extra light. She knew why the cloak of invisibility was there. She knew why the princess's smile held a touch of sadness. She knew why the painting was so special to Granny, and why Granny didn't talk about it very much. She knew why it was called *Farewell*.

Robert Belairs had made the sketch for this painting the night he and Princess Jessica ran away. Before they left the Realm, they had visited the Finding Pool secretly, one last time, knowing they might never see it again.

"If they'd stayed just a few hours longer, they might have seen the sprites find the Moon Stone,

Flynn," Jessie said aloud. "It was found the very next morning, and—"

Then, it was as if a light blazed in her mind. She gasped, hardly able to believe what she was thinking. But it was true! She knew it was! Suddenly she realized why Patrice's description of the Moon Stone had made her feel she'd actually seen it. Jessie *had* seen it—or something very like it.

Her hands trembling, she threw open the lid of the carved chest. She burrowed through crocheted rugs and folded blankets till she found what she was looking for.

The dress lay right at the bottom of the chest, wrapped in tissue paper and scented with lavender. It was exquisite: faded to pale blue-gray but soft as a spiderweb, a dress still fit for a princess though it was over half a century old.

Looped around the waist of the dress was a plaited silver cord. At one end of the cord was a large, misty blue bead, enclosed and held in place by silver netting. At the other end of the cord, only a torn piece of netting remained, hanging loose and empty.

"The Moon Stone didn't appear in the Finding

Pool by magic, Flynn," Jessie breathed. "It was just a decoration that fell from the tie of Granny's dress, into the pool, the night she left the Realm."

Flynn purred, watching her with interest.

Carefully Jessie gathered up the silver cord and took the remaining blue bead between her fingers. The fragile old netting that enclosed it parted and fell away. The blue bead rolled into the palm of her hand.

"When Granny showed me this dress, after I found out who she really was, she said it was mine to keep, if I ever had a use for it," Jessie said to Flynn. "Do you think she really meant it?"

Flynn seemed to nod. And Jessie knew, anyway, that if her grandmother had been there, she would have given the blue bead with all her heart, if it would bring peace to the Realm.

Holding the bead tightly in her hand, she quickly put the rugs and blankets back into the chest and closed the lid. She ran to the door and turned off the light. Then, her head buzzing with plans, she hurried to her own room to change into jeans and a long-sleeved sweater. It would be cold at the Finding Pool tonight.

CHAPTER NINE

Race Against Time

Even sooner than she had hoped, Jessie was back in the Realm, running to the palace. Everything was going according to plan. Her only problem now was how to find her way back to the Finding Pool in the dark.

Her mother had gone next door straight after dinner, determined to make Mrs. Tweedie remember every single thing she'd done that morning.

"It's a nuisance, but I just have to make her retrace her steps till she finds that ring," Rosemary had said as she and Jessie finished clearing the table. "I don't care if it takes all night. She's going around accusing Alf Wiseman of stealing!"

"I know," Jessie had answered. "But surely no one will believe her, Mum. She hasn't got any proof—she admits that herself."

"Proof doesn't matter to some people," Rosemary had said grimly. "And mud sticks, Jessie. A rumor like this could ruin Alf's business. If the ring's found later on, a lot of people will never hear about it. But they'll remember the rumor. And who wants a window cleaner who might—just might—be a thief?"

Jessie hadn't thought about Mr. Wiseman's business. She'd just thought how horrible it would be to be accused of stealing when you were completely innocent.

I'm not surprised the people of Lirralee were angry when the sprites insisted that one of them was a thief, she thought, as the golden lights of the palace came into view. I'd have been angry, too. But Gem, Pip, and Bubbles still shouldn't have blocked the stream. That just made everything worse.

She saw a troop of guards just disappearing down the side of the palace. She ran faster, to catch up. "Are—are you on your way to the Finding Pool?" she said, gasping, to the last two in line.

"We are," said the one on the left without looking around or breaking stride. "They called for reinforcements a few minutes ago. Bit of trouble there, apparently. More than Loris's troop can handle, anyway."

"You'd better go and sit down, miss," put in the other guard, peering at Jessie curiously. "You're very red in the face, if you don't mind my saying so."

"I've been running," Jessie panted. "Listen, I have to get to the Finding Pool myself, but I'm not sure of the way. Can I come with you?"

"Certainly not!" growled the first guard severely. "We've declared the whole forest out of bounds, till we get the situation under control."

"But—but I'm on a mission for Queen Jessica," Jessie stammered, telling herself that this was almost true. "It's really important."

"Oh!" said the second guard, clearly very impressed. "Well, if the true queen sent you, there's no more to be said. Get in between us, miss. We'll see you complete your mission safely."

In moments, Jessie was marching between them into the forest. Soon, she could hear the sound of angry voices and see lights flickering. And shortly after that, her head whirling, she was hurrying through the last of the trees that guarded the Finding Pool.

Torches blazed on the bank near the mouth of the stream, where armed, angry Lirralee people were being held back by exhausted-looking guards. Patrice, with Maybelle on one side and Giff on the other, was facing the crowd, pleading with them to leave. But even Uncle Bon was shaking his head, refusing to move.

The pool itself seemed completely deserted. But then Jessie saw that the reeds in the center were gleaming with eyes, and the points of crystal knives.

She forced her way through the crowd and ran to Patrice's side. She faced the pool, and held up her closed hand.

"Birdwing! Bright-Light-on-Water!" she shouted. "There is no need for you to keep Jewel any longer! I have done what you asked! I have found the Moon Stone!"

There was a moment's breathless silence. Jessie met Patrice's astonished eyes and heard Giff whispering questions, but didn't say a word. Her hand tightened around the blue bead. She waited.

The water at her feet rippled. The tall figure of Bright-Light-on-Water rose from the depths, his long green hair trailing over his shoulders like water weed.

Jessie lowered her hand, opened it, and showed him the blue bead. His eyes seemed to flash with triumph, and he reached out. Jessie drew her hand away. "Bring Jewel," she said softly.

The sprite stared for a moment, then nodded and stirred the surface of the water. It must have been some sort of signal, for at once the reeds in the center of the pool parted, and Cool-of-the-Evening came gliding toward them, pushing Jewel's cradle before her.

Jessie heard Lily and Gem cry out. She heard Giff cheering and Patrice's shout of joy. But she didn't turn around. It wasn't time to rejoice yet. Tensely she watched as the cradle came closer. Soon it was so close that she could see Jewel inside. The baby was fast asleep, her tiny fingers curled round the tail of the little blue and white spotted fish.

The cradle had almost reached Bright-Light-on-Water when the water beside him stirred and another pale figure rose to the surface. It was Birdwing, his face shining with joy. "Show me," he said eagerly, and Jessie held out her hand again and opened it to show the misty blue bead.

The old sprite stared. His brow wrinkled. Then his eyes darkened, like water when a cloud covers the sun. He flicked the pool's surface with one finger, and Cool-of-the-Evening froze behind him.

"This is not the Moon Stone," Birdwing said, his voice trembling. "It is very like, but it is not the same. It is a fraud. They have tried to deceive us!"

Bright-Light-on-Water gave a shout of rage. "Cool-of-the-Evening, return the child to the reeds," he snarled. "I swear that these miserable, lying Lirraleans will never see her again."

Jessie heard a furious shout behind her. Then she was knocked sideways as someone leaped past her and plunged into the water.

Screams rang in her ears as she staggered to

her feet. Her head spinning, she saw a terrible upheaval in the pool. Birdwing had disappeared. Gem was struggling with Bright-Light-on-Water, who was holding him back with a disdainful smile. Gem was gasping, choking, churning the water to foam as he tried to get to Jewel.

"Help him!" howled Pip and Bubbles together. The crowd roared and surged forward. The guards groaned with the effort of holding them back.

"Wait!" Jessie screamed. "Birdwing, wherever you are, listen, please! I was the one who tried to trick you. No one else knew anything about it."

She scanned the water, but could see no sign of the sprite's leader. Despair swept over her, but she made herself go on. "Before you found it, the Moon Stone belonged to my grandmother — Queen Jessica," she called. "It was one of two. I found the second one, and hoped you would accept it, in place of the stone you lost. I thought it was the best thing to do, but I was wrong. Please forgive me!"

A shower of water sprayed up from the pool, blinding her and drenching her to the skin. When at last her eyes cleared, Gem lay spluttering on the grass at her feet, Bright-Light-on-Water was standing as still as a stone in the water, and Birdwing was leaning against the edge of the pool, looking up at her.

"You are as daring and warm-hearted as your grandmother, Princess Jessie," said Birdwing quietly. "But your human blood has caused you to make an error she would never have made. You should not have tried to deceive us."

"I know," Jessie whispered, filled with shame. "Granny would have told me that, I suppose. But she was away from home."

"Now, I fear, there is no chance that Jewel will be returned," Birdwing went on. "Bright-Light-on-Water will see to that. And I will not dare to go against him, for my people would see that as weakness and lose their faith in me."

Jessie felt a flare of anger. "Birdwing, the Moon Stone is just a bead from the tie of Granny's dress!" she whispered fiercely. "It isn't magic! It's just not worth all this misery!"

"Wherever the Moon Stone came from, it is magic to us," Birdwing said calmly. "Our belief makes it so. You do not understand. You are the granddaughter of Queen Jessica, my child, but you think as humans think."

He's right, Jessie thought dismally. And at that moment, an idea flashed into her mind—an idea put there by that most practical of humans, her mother. She clenched her fists "What if I found the real Moon Stone?" she demanded. "What then?"

"Why, then, I daresay, everything would be different," Birdwing said slowly. "But you have already told us that the task is impossible."

"Well, I've changed my mind," Jessie said. "Listen, Birdwing. Everyone who was here on the night the Moon Stone disappeared is also here tonight. That's right, isn't it?"

"Yes," the old sprite said. "What of it?"

Jessie told him. He listened carefully as she spoke, and when she had finished he nodded slowly.

"It is an interesting idea," he said. "Everything as it was. Someone might notice something they did not notice before. The thief may be unmasked. Very well, then. We will try."

CHAPTER TEN

Just as it was

Half an hour later, the Finding Pool was quiet. The guards, Patrice, Maybelle, and Giff had retreated to the forest. Jewel's cradle was again hidden in the reeds. The people of Lirralee were nowhere to be seen.

Birdwing had moved to the muddy edge of the flat part of the Finding Pool where Jessie had first met the mud wubbles. In front of him was a large treasure chest. Bright-Light-on-Water was beside him, a long, thin pouch slung over one shoulder. The other sprites were clustered in the shallow water behind them. Everyone was looking at Jessie.

"All right," Jessie said nervously. "You're all just where you were before the Lirralee people came on the night the Moon Stone disappeared. What happened then?"

Birdwing bent and took from the chest the blue stone that Jessie had brought to the pool.

"Okay," said Jessie. "So Birdwing has the Moon Stone."

"That is not the Moon Stone," Bright-Light-on-Water spat.

"It's the same size and shape, and it will do for the experiment," Jessie said patiently. "Now, what next?"

"Bright-Light-on-Water played the Finding Flute!" a sprite child piped from the back.

"I will not do it," Bright-Light-on-Water said. "The Finding Flute has not been played since the Moon Stone was lost and must not be played again until it is found."

Jessie sighed. "Then just pretend to play it," she said.

Sullenly, Bright-Light-on-Water drew a muddy, neglected-looking wooden flute from the pouch. He put it to his lips and pretended to play.

"After that, we remained in these places until the Lirralee folk came," Birdwing said quietly. "That is always how it is done. The flute is played all through the return."

Jessie nodded. "Uncle Bon!" she called. "Bring everyone to the pool!"

The Lirralee people came trailing from behind the bushes that clustered at the mouth of the stream. Unsmiling, they trudged to where the water sprites waited. They grouped themselves not far from the treasure chest, shaking jeering mud wubbles from their boots.

"Now—everything just as it was," said Jessie.

Birdwing nodded. With great ceremony, he passed the blue bead to Bright-Light-on-Water, who put it into the pouch around his neck and then began pretending to play the flute again.

One by one, the Lirralee people came forward, looked into the empty treasure chest, and pretended to take something away. The minutes dragged by. Jessie's spirits sank. This isn't going to work, she thought.

"Well, we've learned something, anyway," growled Gem at last. "The bead has been in the flute pouch all this time. I'd like someone to tell me how one of *us* stole it!"

"If you ask me, Bright-Light-on-Water has some explaining to do," called Bubbles loudly.

"Yes," called Pip. "Maybe he wanted to take over from Birdwing so much that he didn't mind stirring up a bit of trouble to help him do it!"

"How dare you!" snarled Bright-Light-on-Water, taking a step forward.

"Stay where you are, Bright-Light-on-Water," said Birdwing quietly. "Bon of Lirralee, you came to the treasure chest last, I think?"

Jessie watched in despair as Uncle Bon trudged to the chest, pretended to dip his hand into it, then trudged away again.

"That's wrong!" called the sprite child from the back. "That's not how it was! The mud wubbles tripped the fat one. He fell into the water. He made a big, huge splash. Everyone laughed."

The other sprite children giggled. The people of Lirralee glowered.

"That's true," said Uncle Bon with dignity. "I'd forgotten. But I don't particularly want to fall in now, if you don't mind."

"I would much prefer you did not," said Birdwing. "The wave you made threw Bright-Light-on-Water and me down onto the bank, as I recall. The mud wubbles were very gleeful. They would not let us rise for quite a time."

"Please!" cried Jessie. "Please, act it out as exactly as you can. We've nearly finished, but we have to do this properly."

"Oh, very well." Uncle Bon sighed. He pretended to slip and splashed into the water. Birdwing fell to the ground. Bright-Light-on-Water did the same. Gurgling joyfully, mud wubbles began swarming all over them, covering them with sticky mud. Gem hurried past them, slipped, fell to his knees, then staggered up and began pulling Uncle Bon from the water.

Bright-Light-on-Water shoved the Finding Flute back into its pouch, fought off the mud wubbles and got to his feet. He bent to Birdwing, and helped the old sprite up. Both of them were covered in mud, but Bright-Light-on-Water's eyes were sparkling.

"This experiment was worthwhile after all," he said. "I see now how the Moon Stone was stolen.

It must have rolled from the pouch when I fell."

"You mean—the mud wubbles took it?" Jessie gasped.

Bright-Light-on-Water shook his head. "No doubt they would think it a great joke," he said. "But they are too stupid to hide the Moon Stone from us for long. No. Someone saw it and snatched it up. And there was only one person who had the chance to do that. The one who pretended to fall beside me while I was down." His hand darted out, and fastened on Gem's arm.

"No!" cried Lily, running forward. "Let him go!"

"I didn't do anything," Gem roared, tearing his arm free. "Why would I take your wretched stone?"

But Jessie could think of a reason. The Moon Stone was supposed to bring good fortune. Lily and Gem wanted a child very badly. Gem was impulsive. He might have . . .

"This is a mistake," said Uncle Bon loyally. But his eyes were anxious. Jessie could see that he had the same doubts as she did.

"I fear it is not," said Birdwing. "Straight after

this, your people began to leave us. Bright-Light-on-Water and I were caked in mud, as we are now. I told him to return the Moon Stone to the treasure chest so that we could enter the water once more. It was then we discovered that the Moon Stone had gone. There was nothing inside the pouch but mud."

Jessie's heart leaped. She'd just thought of something. "Bright-Light-on-Water, act it out," she said urgently. "Put the stone back in the treasure chest."

With a disdainful snort, Bright-Light-on-Water pulled the Finding Flute from the pouch. He turned the pouch upside down. Nothing fell out. His jaw dropped. He pulled the pouch inside out. There was nothing inside but mud.

"How can this be?" Birdwing gasped, as everyone else exclaimed in wonder. "Is the pouch bewitched?"

"Could I hold the Finding Flute for a moment?" Jessie asked.

Too stunned to protest, Bright-Light-on-Water passed it to her. Jessie tapped the end of the flute against the palm of her hand. Nothing happened.

She tapped again, a little harder. A plug of wet mud oozed out, followed by a round blue bead.

The water sprites exclaimed. The people of Lirralee roared. But Jessie wasn't finished. Again she tapped the tip of the flute. A shower of dried mud fell out. And then, suddenly, there was a rattling sound, and into the palm of her hand rolled another blue bead, just like the first.

"There," Jessie said with satisfaction, as everyone cheered.

"I cannot believe this!" Birdwing shook his head. "The Moon Stone was not stolen. It was in the Finding Flute, all the time!"

"Yes," said Jessie, grinning. "And it was all because of the mud wubbles. Like my mum says: mud sticks."

"So, when Bright-Light-on-Water was trying to get up out of the mud, he jammed the Finding Flute into its pouch, on top of the Moon Stone," Jessie told her grandmother the next day, as they drank hot chocolate in the Blue Moon kitchen. "The Moon Stone went into the end of the Flute.

That wouldn't have mattered, except for the mud that the mud wubbles had put in the pouch. It jammed the Moon Stone inside the Flute—just as it did the second time, with the other blue bead."

"I'm surprised that Bright-Light-on-Water didn't notice that the flute was heavier than it should have been," Granny said, with a puzzled frown.

"He was so angry I doubt he'd have noticed anything," Jessie said. "Anyway, he feels very silly now. He won't be giving Birdwing any more trouble for a while."

She licked chocolate from her lips and admired the new charm hanging from her bracelet. It had appeared on her desk that morning—a tiny golden flute.

"So all's well." She sighed happily. "The sprites have apologized to the Lirralee people for suspecting them; I've apologized for taking away the net; Gem, Pip, and Bubbles have apologized for damming the stream; and Jewel's back in Lirralee. Everyone's happy—except the mud wubbles."

Granny laughed. "All's well here, too, I gather,"

she said. "I saw Louise Tweedie as I came in. She said she'd found her ring—under the telephone, of all places! But she didn't tell me much else."

"She's probably embarrassed," Jessie said. "Mum made her act out everything she'd done yesterday morning. She suddenly remembered that the phone had rung while she was on her way to put her ring in its usual place. So they looked at the phone, and Mum lifted it up, and there was the ring! Mrs. Tweedie must have put it down while she was talking, and it had slipped underneath the phone somehow. When she hung up, she obviously just went off to do the washing, and forgot all about it."

"She was very grateful, anyway," Granny said, her eyes twinkling. "She said the way Rosemary found her ring was just like magic. But it wasn't magic, was it?"

Jessie grinned, and shook her head. "Not this time, Granny," she said. "This time, it was just human common sense."

Turn the page for a peek at
Jessie's next adventure in the

Fairy Realm:

BOOK 9

The peskie spell

It was a fine, sunny Sunday, but a wild wind blew around the old house called Blue Moon, rattling the windows and tossing the branches of the trees. Red and yellow leaves swirled in the air like flocks of small, bright birds.

Inside the house, Jessie glanced up at the leaves flying past the high windows of her grandfather's studio. She felt jumpy and uneasy. She was supposed to be dusting a pile of sketchbooks she'd taken from a glass-fronted cabinet, but she just couldn't concentrate.

"This is what Granny calls 'pesky weather,'" she said to her mother, who was sweeping the studio floor. "Remember that song she always sings when it's sunny and windy both at the same time?"

Rosemary smiled and began to sing, moving her broom in time to the music:

"Pesky weather, nothing goes right!
Pesky weather, lock the doors tight!

Make a magic brew,
With seven drops of dew,
A drop of thistle milk,
And a strand of spider silk . . ."

She broke off, laughing. "Well, things have gone right for us today, Jess, in spite of the pesky weather," she said. "The studio's looking pretty good, now. It'll just need a quick dust before the photographer comes on Thursday."

"Will Granny be home by then?" Jessie asked. Her grandmother was away seeing some people at the National Gallery who were organizing a big exhibition of her late husband's famous fairy paintings. The exhibition was to be held in a few months' time, and a photograph of the Blue Moon studio was going to be part of it.

"Oh, yes," Rosemary said. "She'll be back on Tuesday night. How are you going with those sketchbooks, Jess?"

"Nearly finished," said Jessie hastily. She knew she'd been spending more time looking at the books than cleaning them. The one she was holding now was filled with sketches of trees, leaves, and flowers, and she'd found some real flowers pressed between the pages, too: forget-me-nots, violets, and many other flowers she didn't know.

"Can I borrow this one, Mum?" she asked, holding up the book.

"Sure," her mother said. "Just be careful with it. And don't take it outside."

Jessie put the sketchbook on top of the glass-fronted cabinet and went on dusting the other books and stacking them away.

It was her grandfather's fairy paintings that had made him famous, but he'd painted land-scapes, trees, flowers, birds, and animals, too. People who saw his sketchbooks were always fascinated. "What an imagination Robert Belairs had," they'd say. "It's just as if fantasy creatures like griffins and mermaids were just as real to him as lizards and cockatoos!"

Little did they know that there was a very good reason for this—the best reason in the world. Jessie's grandfather had seen griffins and mermaids and other strange beings with his own eyes.

He'd seen them in the magical world of the Realm, after he discovered an invisible Door at the bottom of the Blue Moon garden. For years he'd brought back sketches from the Realm. Then, one day, he'd brought back something else: the Realm princess called Jessica, who was to become his wife, Rosemary's mother, and Jessie's very special grandmother.

Only Jessie shared Granny's secret. She'd discovered it by accident and had promised to keep it. She knew she couldn't tell anyone about the Realm. But how she'd have loved to talk about it with her mother, with her best friend, Sal—and even with her schoolteacher, Ms. Stone, who was always criticizing her for writing about magical things instead of what Ms. Stone called "real life"!

If only she could tell them about the Realm— and about her friends Giff the elf, Maybelle the miniature horse, Patrice the palace housekeeper, and Queen Helena, who ruled the Realm in her sister Jessica's place! If only she could tell them that every charm on the gold bracelet now jingling softly on her wrist was a gift from the Realm to remind her of an exciting adventure.

The Realm . . .

Jessie frowned. Thoughts of the Realm had brought back the restless, uneasy feeling and now it was stronger than ever.

"Jessie, is something wrong?"

Jessie looked up quickly, meeting her mother's puzzled eyes. "You've obviously got something on your mind," Rosemary said. "Is Ms. Stone giving you trouble at school again?"

Jessie forced a smile. "No," she said. "Ms. Stone's concentrating on Lisa Wells and Rachel Lew at the moment. She followed them up from the parking lot on Friday morning and saw that they were jumping over all the cracks in the path. When she asked them why, they said it was because stepping on a crack was bad luck." Despite herself, she giggled.

Rosemary laughed with her. "I can just imagine what Ms. Stone said about *that*!" she said, turning back to her sweeping.

"Yeah," said Jessie. "In class she went on for ages about how stupid it was to believe in things like that. Then she asked everyone to tell her all the sayings about bad luck they knew. She wrote them down and said that on Monday she was going to prove that none of them is true."

Rosemary shook her head. "Your Ms. Stone's really got a bee in her bonnet about make-believe, hasn't she?" she said. "It's as if she's on a one-woman quest to stamp it out. She's right about superstitions being silly, of course. But she won't be able to *prove* it. In fact—"

"Yoo-hoo!" called a voice from the back door. "It's only me."

Jessie and her mother exchanged rueful glances. "Come in, Louise," Rosemary called back. "We're in the studio."

Mrs. Tweedie, their next-door neighbor, appeared at the studio door. Her spiky gray hair had been blown about by the wind, and her pointed nose was bright red at the tip. Flynn, Granny's big orange cat, was stalking behind her, looking very disapproving.

"I won't disturb you," said Mrs. Tweedie, bustling into the room. "I just popped in to bring you a few fruit slices I made this morning. They're on the kitchen table."

"Oh—thank you, Louise," Rosemary said. "You are kind."

It's just an excuse to come in here and poke around, Jessie thought crossly. Then she felt a bit mean. Obviously Mrs. Tweedie was lonely. She was avid for details about other peoples' lives because she didn't have any life of her own.

Mrs. Tweedie began wandering around the studio, her sharp, birdlike eyes darting everywhere. "Have you heard from your mother today yet, Rosemary?" she asked, stopping at the glass-fronted cabinet and beginning to leaf through the sketchbook lying there.

"We won't be hearing from her again till Tuesday," said Rosemary. "Her next meeting isn't till then, so she's gone off on a bird-watching camp with some group she met at the gallery."

"Really?" gushed Mrs. Tweedie. "Oh, isn't she *marvelous.*"

"Marvelous," Rosemary agreed dryly. "But I wish she'd agree to get a mobile phone. Well,

Louise, we'd better—"

"Oh!" squealed Mrs. Tweedie, bending over the sketchbook. "Oh, look what I've found! A pressed flower—perfectly preserved! I even caught a whiff of its scent as I turned the page. Jessie, look at this!"

Jessie bit her tongue to stop herself saying that the sketchbook had *dozens* of pressed flowers in it, and that there was no need for Mrs. Tweedie to make such a fuss.

But her irritation was replaced by sheer panic when she saw what Mrs. Tweedie was looking at. The flower was as delicate as if it were made of fairy wings. Despite its age, its center was still bright yellow and its petals were a beautiful blue.

Jessie knew without doubt that this was a flower from the Realm. She'd never seen it before, but there was something about it that breathed magic. How like her grandfather to have put it in the book with perfectly ordinary flowers from the Blue Moon garden! And what bad luck that Mrs. Tweedie had seen it!

"What sort of flower do you think it is?" Mrs.

Tweedie twittered. "It's *most* unusual."

"It's just a blue daisy, isn't it?" said Jessie, trying to keep her voice even.

"Oh, I don't think so," said Mrs. Tweedie, putting her head on one side. She whirled around to Rosemary and clasped her hands. "I know it's a lot to ask," she said breathlessly, "but could I borrow this flower for a teeny while? I'd love to try to identify it."

Jessie held her breath, then felt a wave of relief as her mother looked embarrassed and shook her head. "I'm awfully sorry, Louise," Rosemary said, "but Dad's sketchbooks and all their contents are— well, rather precious. I don't think it would be right to let anything leave the house—at least while Mum's away. I hope you understand."

Mrs. Tweedie flushed slightly. "Oh—of course!" she said in rather a high voice. "Of course. Well. I'd better be going. Don't bother to see me out. I know my way."

She waved clumsily and hurried from the room. Flynn got up and padded after her, as if he was seeing her off the premises.

"Oh dear! Now I've hurt her feelings," Rosemary said as the back door slammed.

"You were perfectly right, Mum!" said Jessie vehemently.

Rosemary smiled and shrugged. "Look, I'll finish up here, Jessie," she said. "You go on outside. I know you're dying to get out into the pesky weather, and the fresh air might do you good. Just be indoors by sunset. All right?"

"All right!" Jessie promised gladly.

She took the sketchbook to her room. She pulled on a jacket, and was just about to rush out again when she thought of something. She grabbed an old gray cloak from the top of her wardrobe and stuffed it into her school backpack.

A minute later she was outside, the pack on her back, her long red hair whipping in the wind. She glanced over her shoulder to make sure that Mrs. Tweedie wasn't watching over the fence, then ran for the secret garden.

Soon I'll be in the Realm, she thought. Then I'll know. Then I'll know. . . .

In the secret garden, the rosemary bushes that

edged the little square of green lawn were as fragrant as ever. The high, clipped hedge still seemed to keep the whole world out.

Jessie gave a sigh of relief. "Open!" she said. She closed her eyes and waited for the familiar cool, tingling breeze that always swept over her as she moved into the Realm.

But she didn't feel anything at all. And when she opened her eyes she found that nothing had changed. She was still in the secret garden. Jessie blinked in shock.

"Open!" she repeated unsteadily. But again nothing happened. The magic hadn't worked. The Door to the Realm hadn't opened.

She was locked out.

EMILY RODDA

has written many books for children, including the Rowan of Rin books. She has won the Children's Book Council of Australia Book of the Year Award an unprecedented five times. A former editor, Ms. Rodda is also the bestselling author of adult mysteries under the name Jennifer Rowe. She lives in Australia.